KLEPTO

IT'S THEIR WORLD NOW!

By Daphne Pendergrass

ISBN 978-1-338-29825-3

10 9 8 7 6 5 4 3 2 1   18 19 20 21 22

Printed in the U.S.A.   40
First printing 2018

Book design by Jessica Meltzer
Edited by Samantha Lizzio

TABLE OF CONTENTS

MEET THE MOST DIABOLICAL KLEPTOCATS

Welcome, underling! If you're reading this, it probably means the KleptoCats have entered your life. **Congratulations!** Consider this your one stop shop for info about your new feline overlords. Loyal servants who make it to the end of this book will be **rewarded**. As you know, new cats join the KleptoCats' ranks all the time, so keeping track of your majestic masters can be tricky. In this section, you'll find a list of the most devious, yet adorable, cats you should probably keep an eye on!

GUAPO

- KleptoCats' fearless leader.
- Best thief this side of the Milky Way.
- Brave, smart, and compassionate.
- Led the charge in the Great Hamster War.
- Loves sandwiches and belly rubs.
- Like other KleptoCats, can travel anywhere via mystic portals.
- His furr-ocious meow has inspired nine planetary conquests.

THE BEDROOM CATS

NUBE

- Learned how to open doors.
- Pretty good with a slingshot.

JARED

- Likes to play with its poop.
- Concerned for your well-being.

SAKURA

- Collects items in a hidden space behind the couch.
- Super chill.

CHELL

- Likes to eat ham . . . like, *really* likes it.
- Terrified of bacon.

FÁYER

- Mouse-stached adventurer. It doesn't like people that much.

- Will tell your fortune in return for fresh tuna.

GREEN

- Don't make it angry. You won't like it when it's angry.

- Sleeps with its butt in the air.

GHOST

- Haunts other cats for fun.

- Will fart in your face and then float away.

MIME

- Likes to watch you when you sleep.

- Trapped in an invisible box.

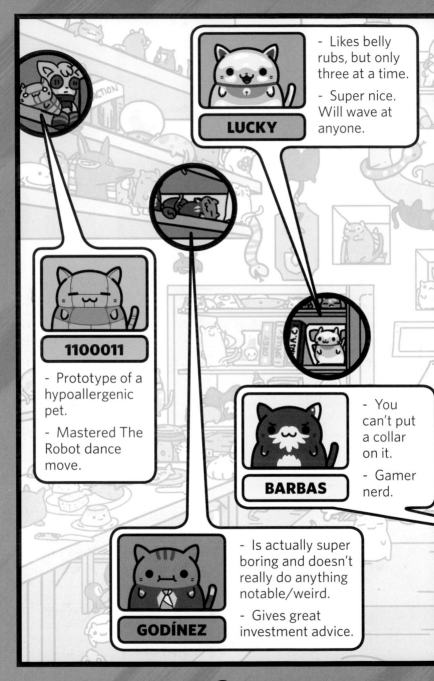

MORADA
- Its favorite color is "purrple."
- Loves turtles.

WERO
- Befriended a mouse once.
- Still hates cheese.

DAVID
- Likes to look at the stars in a melancholic way.
- Jams with spiders.

PRINCESS
- Hates it when you touch its tail.
- Set to inherit a planet in a distant galaxy.

NEAL D.

- Enjoys ruining your favorite movie by explaining scientific facts about it.

- Thinks it can fly.

SANDI

- Tried a lemon once and made a silly face.

- Sharpens its claws on the lampshade.

RODRIGA

- Alpha cat.

- Inspires awe in all rodents.

- Is actually an alien in disguise.

- Makes a funny noise when you scratch its ears.

JELLY

BOWTIE

- Looks fancy but likes to drink water from the toilet.
- Loves to lick faces.

ROOTBEER

- Great at multitasking.
- A champion cockroach-catcher.

CLEO

- *Dances like an Egyptian*
- Hid the *Book of the Dead* in the back of the closet.

CLOWNY

- "What do you call a pile of kittens? A 'meowntain'."
- Scared of balloons.

THE PATIO CATS

BUBBLE

- Loves to swim in the sea.
- Draws faces on things when no one is looking.

HARU

- Steals bread from the table.
- Thinks beards are cool.

ANDREA

- Understands you probably more than you do.
- Plays the cello . . . or at least, tries to.

PURRIOSA

- One of its legs is damaged.
- Known for holding grudges.

FABIANA

- Its fur shines bright like diamonds.
- Loves seafood.

RENATA

- Meows in French.
- Scared of heights.

MARMS

- Looks evil, but it's so cute.
- Attracted to shiny objects.

PIXEL

- Other cats envy its fur.
- Don't give it sugar.

THE CHAMBER CATS

OLI

- Loves pig in all its presentations.
- Sometimes starts fires to feel alive.

LUPITO

- It's always showing off its muscles.
- Doesn't trust guinea pigs.

BERNARDO

- Gets scared by its own farts.
- Likes long car rides.

CONCHITA

- Licks your elbow if you are distracted.
- Feels superior since you can't lick your elbow.

CARBONO

- Glows in the dark.

- Fell down the stairs once . . . in the dark.

JEN

- Very fancy cat—only eats fresh tuna, not the canned kind.

- For more information on fancy cats, see page 90.

NUNU

- Enjoys writing and reading creepy stories.

- Doesn't react well to criticism.

OSCURO

- Complains a lot on the Internet.

- Goes by the username Anony-meows.

THE LIBRARY CATS

DIANA

- Likes to educate the other cats.
- Went to Paris once.

HAVOC

- Starts fights with other cats.
- Has its Halloween costume picked out for the next nine years.

WASABI

- Never goes to bed angry.
- Spicy.

BASILI

- Fly killer.
- Always gets asked to fix the computer.

IWATA

- Always looking for treasures.
- Doesn't like to get its paws dirty though.

16

- Has the strange ability to walk on the ceiling.
- Watch out— its claws are sharp.

COPAL

- Meows in three languages.
- Four if you count Meowrse Code.

JAYSHEE

- Wishes she was a pony.
- But likes unicorns too.

CONNIE

THE HAUNTING CATS

TERRA

- Always getting in the way of people walking.

- Its hiss is the stuff of legends.

JOACHIN

- It was the model in the "hang in there" poster.

- At least, that's what it *wants* you to think.

AQUA

- Learned how to rub its own belly.

- Still needs a back scratcher.

ATREYU

- Hide-and-seek champion.

- Wanted for yarn theft in three states.

THE HOLIDAY CATS

PANNYA

- Cats don't really hibernate, but this one does.

- It hoards cheese puffs to prove it.

YANG

- Doesn't enjoy losing in video games. It's a rage quitter.

- People call it a squeaker, but it's actually much older than you.

VENUS

- It likes to trick people into thinking it is two different cats.

- Only successful in profile.

SPRINKLE

- The sweetest cat you'll ever meet.

- Undefeated Candy Land champion.

THE WASHITSU CATS

CORPORAL

- One day will change its name to General.
- On Guapo's war council.

PUSSANDRA

- Always reaches the highest point in the room.
- Believes someone is watching it.

PEANUT

- Ironically allergic to nuts.
- Got mistaken for a jaguar once.

MIDNIGHT

- Believes it's a dog after seeing a full moon.
- The only cat that's nice to Gemdog.

THE GARAGE CATS

DINO

- RAWR! It scared you. Didn't it?

- Believes it hatched from a three-million-year-old egg.

CITRUS

- Ate too many oranges and now, well . . .

- High in Vitamin C.

MEOWDAM

- Likes to enjoy the finer things in life.

- For more information on fancy cats, see page 90.

SKETCH

- Loves to be around children. Doesn't care if they draw on it.

- Charges $618/hour for babysitting.

THE ATTIC CATS

PEACE

- It's a tree hugger. Total hippy cat.

- Plays the flute.

FELINE

- It covers its poop with sand and twigs.

- Everyone wishes it would just use the litter box.

STAR

- Believes it's destined for stardom.

- Won't sing in front of anyone.

FAUX

- It pretends to be a fox. But it's a cat.

- Crafty though.

THE BACKYARD CATS

PHOTON

- It can be seen hanging upside down in trees.

- Met an alien three weeks ago.

PIÑA

- It enjoys tropical locations.

- Once beat back a zombie horde.

BULLSEYE

- It's really good at darts.

- But really bad at bowling.

QUEST

- It doesn't believe in the dangers of curiosity.

- Holds a Ph.C. (Cat of Philosophy).

THE FIREPLACE CATS

HOOT

- Its eyes are especially piercing.
- It's not the sound you're hearing at 3 a.m.

SE7EN

- It warped here from another dimension.
- The other cats aren't impressed.

GREYEN

- It looks like it's not from around here.
- Moves unbelievably slow.

TANGO

- It likes to dance in the night.
- Hates waiting in line.

SPECIAL . . . CATS?

CATHULHU

- Can be summoned by collecting the KleptoCats Dani, Mara, Tori, and Voxel, in the Patio.

- Don't be alarmed if Cathulhu appears. It and its spawn won't destroy our world for several thousand years yet.

- Its purple glow is from a radioactive element harmful only to fish-folk and fairy creatures.

GEMDOG

- Sometimes a KleptoCat will get distracted and send GemDog back in its place (since he is *very* good at fetch).

- You can always find your cat again in the Cat-alog. GemDog will remain in your room in the meantime (because he's also *very* loyal).

- GemDog has been known to bring . . . a cupcake! Just kidding. He brings you a gem, you silly goose.

CARE, KEEPING, AND COEXISTING WITH KLEPTOCATS

While no one can promise that life with KleptoCats will be comfortable, there are definitely some ways to prevent undue panic. Here are the basics of KleptoCat care and some things to look out for.

FEEDING THE KLEPTOCATS

They'll help themselves to whatever's in the fridge.

They're hungry.

Or just greedy.

Kleptocats will find their own place to sleep. whether that means retrieving their own bed . . .

. . . or helping themselves to yours.

Occasionally, your cats might need a little vacation. Don't worry, they like to stay close to home.

HOW TO MAKE YOUR CATS HAPPY

1. Keep the house well stocked.

2. Don't freak out if they invite guests over.

3. Encourage their less destructive hobbies.

4. They're not always going to use the litter box, but applaud them when they do.

PRACTICAL USES FOR SNAKES

Cat control . . .

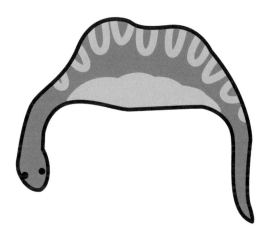

Fitness instructor

Help with Spelling

Sea monster
distraction

STARTING A BUSINESS WITH KLEPTOCATS

Identify an investor.

Get the word out by advertising in the newspaper.

Make Sure they don't eat all of the product.

Rake in the dough.

SOUNDS YOU HEAR AT 3 A.M.

MEEEOOOOOWWWWW

Expectation: Kitten Around

Reality: A-MEOW-rican Idol Audition

THUD!

Expectation: Interior Decorating

Reality: Im-PAW-sible
Escape Attempt

PRIME EXAMPLES OF KLEPTO-CAMOUFLAGE

Snuggly camouflage

underwater camouflage

unSuspecting camouflage

Disguise camouflage

SOLUTIONS TO DESTRUCTIVE HABITS

Destructive Habit:

Scratching things.

Solution:

Put cat in box.

Destructive Habit:

Usually anything involving fire.

Solution:

Water.

Destructive Habit:

Throwing weapons.

Solution:

Use a shield.

Destructive Habit:

Bringing home explosives.

Solution:

Try an interdimensional portal!

AWESOME THINGS YOUR KLEPTOCATS WILL BRING!

Now that you're past the initial panic that comes with a home full of interdimensional, kleptomaniac overlords, let's look at the fun side—all the awesome things that your KleptoCats will bring you.

Ranging from the wildly fantastic to the most mundane, the KleptoCats will often bring you things you never thought possible—and also stuff that will leave you wondering why on earth they'd bring you this.

But first, here's a reflection of you.
Don't forget . . . it's their world now.

THINGS THAT MIGHT GIVE YOU NIGHTMARES

This collection of masks that's totally not staring at you

   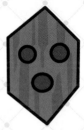

whatever this is . . .

Scorpions . . . on the ceiling . . .

That thing watching you through
the library window . . .

KLEPTOCATS' BOOK CLUB

This might explain the excessive amount of throwing stars they bring back, but not the snakes.

I wonder if this is how Kleptocats get their magical stealing abilities.

Just do what the book says.
Your safety depends on it.

Tip #1: Obey your cat. Wait a
minute . . . I'm Sensing a theme here.

Guinea pigs are devious creatures—just like hamsters. They cannot be trusted with their fat furry faces.

This book has all the must know information about the Ancient Guardians. They brought back another little guy today. It's unclear what they're guarding.

The Young Poisoner's Handbook—how peculiar! Best watch your food.

"Mew mew meow. Purrrr, mew. Mrooooww." = Look away as I lick my butt.

KLEPTOCATS' MOST COMMON HOUSEGUESTS

Confused Woodland Creatures

Extraterrestrials . . . or their remains . . .

Dogs

More snakes . . . Seriously, what is it with the snakes?

KLEPTOCATS' GUIDE TO INTERIOR DECORATING

Step 1. Hang pictures of your many conquests.

Step 2. If you can't find a shelf, make one.

Step 3. Candles can add a romantic touch to any room.

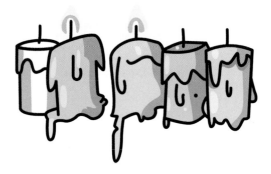

Step 4. Hang Stuff from the ceiling! Doesn't really matter what.

WHAT'S HOT THIS FASHION SEASON, AS TOLD BY KLEPTOCATS

IN: Hats with eyes

Out: Hats with eyeholes

IN: Yarn

Out: Sweaters

KLEPTOCATS' GUIDE TO SELF-IMPROVEMENT

Eat healthy!

Expectation:

Reality:

Try new things! Like gardening!

Expectation:

Reality:

KLEPTOCATS' GUIDE TO CLEANLINESS

Sometimes, spills can be delicious.

There is a trash can, but they're not sure what it's for.

Not all brooms are meant for cleaning. Sweeping is for humans.

SIGNS THAT YOUR CATS ARE UP TO SOMETHING

They're building a decoy cat that looks oddly similar to a wanted poster.

There's a video feed of that octocat thing they like attacking someone.

They're amassing weapons.

There are skeletons in the walls.

TRANSLATING YOUR KLEPTOCAT'S GIFTS

GIFT:
Small dead animals.

TRANSLATION:
We're out of Bagel Bites.

GIFT:
Shadow men.

TRANSLATION:
They're just throwing you shade.

GIFT:
A tree covered with string.

TRANSLATION:
We saw this and thought of you! A.K.A.: we have no idea what you like.

GIFT:
Ambivalent ghosts.

TRANSLATION:
You were looking lonely, so we brought friends.

PLEASING YOUR NEW OVERLORDS

We're guessing you've never had to ensure the happiness of portal-jumping, interdimensional cats before, but fear not! This section will get you in tip-top shape for all your duties as the proud servant of these benevolent beings.

You can start by reading their new novel. Don't worry. You've definitely got the time.

INTERPRETING THE MANY MOODS OF KLEPTOCATS

Supreme Happiness

Surprised

Definitely Not up to Something

"He Did It!"

Too Beautiful for This World

Tummy Troubles

Peaceful

Busy—Come Back Later

DOS AND DON'TS OF GROOMING

Do:

Don't:

Do:

Don't:

HOW TO BATHE KLEPTOCATS

1. Catch a Stinky Kleptocat.

2. Get Soap.

3. Scrub gently until no longer stinky.

4. So beautiful!

TREAT-WORTHY BEHAVIOR

Cheating death

Building Something

Saying no to bad behavior

Fetching (Just don't use the word "Fetch"; KleptoCats hate that.)

STAGES OF HUNGER

I wants food.

I has food.

I eats ALL the food.

. . .

SURVIVING THE HOLIDAYS WITH KLEPTOCATS

Don't let them outside.

Don't let them decorate.

Don't show them the cookie jar.

Don't tell them about Santa.

KLEPTOCATS' FOOD GROUPS

Grains

Meats

Fats

Pizza

CARING FOR FANCY KLEPTOCATS

1. Don't be late for tea.

2. Dress them in only the finest jewelry.

3. Acknowledge their more sophisticated meows.

4. Share in their artistic tastes.

CARING FOR AWKWARD KLEPTOCATS

1. Note the longer processing time.

2. Encourage them to make friends, even if those friends aren't . . . alive.

3. Don't let them lick you.

4. If your derpy Kleptocat freezes, just wait for it to reset.

HOW TO PROPERLY PET KLEPTOCATS

1. Get a tired Kleptocat.

2. Pet its head really fast.

3. Let it soak up the love.

4. Don't pet it again or you'll ruin it.

WELL DONE, UNDERLING!

You've made it to the end of this book. We hope you found this guide to the KleptoCats informative and fun. Best of luck to you in serving your new masters!

Decipher this code, solve the clue, and enter the answer in the game safe in KleptoCats or KleptoCats 2 for some extra help in your mission.

(32, 4, 4)

(4, 8, 5)

(87, 3, 3)

(58, 6, 4)

(54, 4, 6)

(38, 4, 1)

(73, 6, 1)

(5, 1, 3)